This Igloo book belongs to:

...............................................

# igloo

Published in 2010
by Igloo Books Ltd
Cottage Farm
Sywell
Northants
NN6 0BJ
www.igloo-books.com

10 9 8 7 6 5 4 3
ISBN: 978-0-85734-152-5

Printed and manufactured in China

Illustrated by Leo Brown
Stories by Joff Brown

# ❧ Contents ☙

# Night of the Full Moon

It was a cold, dark, night and the Brown family were lost. Their car had juddered to a halt outside the gates of a large country house. Mr Brown shook his head in disbelief. "We'll just have to ask for help at that old house," said Mrs Brown. In the back of the car, their two sons, Ed and Matthew, rolled their eyes, as if they were really bored by the idea.

A few moments later, the Browns stood in the crumbling porch of Upshire Hall. "Can I ring the bell?" said Matthew, reaching out and tugging an old-fashioned bell-pull. A deep, mournful ringing sound echoed from beyond the door. The Brown family looked at one another.

"What a weird noise," said Ed, looking up at the grim walls of the foreboding house. "The mad butler is going to open the door any minute. We're all going to die!"
"Be quiet," shushed Mrs. Brown, "someone's coming."

Footsteps echoed from inside. The huge, oak door creaked open. An elderly man stood in the doorway, holding a dusty old candelabra. "Good evening," he said, "I didn't expect any visitors, especially not tonight. I'm Lord Upshire. Do come in, it's not safe out there."

"What does he mean, 'not safe'?" whispered Mrs Brown, as the family shuffled inside. Suits of armour lined the walls and the hall had the smell and feel of somewhere that had been long neglected.

"Sorry to trouble you, My Lord," said Mr. Brown. "I wondered if I might use your phone? Our car just stopped suddenly, right outside the gates of your house.

Lord Upshire nodded, knowingly. "It's the moon," he said. "Strange things always happen here when there's a full moon. Nothing will work until tomorrow, I'm afraid, no phones and no electricity. The place is cursed, you know. Even the staff have left. It's just me here, now." He lifted the candelabra and the candles flickered dimly around the bleak hall.

Lord Upshire shrugged his shoulders and smiled. "You'll all have to stay here tonight. I can't let you go wandering off outside, the cats will be out soon." The Brown family glanced at each other. Why should cats be a problem?

After something to eat, Lord Upshire showed the family to their rooms. "You must bolt your door," he warned the boys. "Do *not* open it under *any* circumstances." Then he handed them a candle and shuffled off to bed.

Ed and Matthew's room was creepy and smelled of mushrooms, like an ancient museum. The sheets were cold and the boys were too scared to close their eyes. Suddenly, there was a noise outside, in the hallway. The boys sat bolt upright in bed. The noise was a throaty, gurgling, growl.

Despite Lord Upshire's warning, Ed opened the door and the boys peered down the gloomy corridor. There was nothing there. The noise came again, this time it was further away. "It's coming from the long gallery," said Matthew. The brothers crept slowly forwards and the candle flickered eerily in the damp, drafty hallway.

The gallery was silent. Around the room and on the walls, the stuffed bodies and heads of big cats glared silently. "It's like a dead jungle," whispered Matthew.

Suddenly, something moved on the floor by the fireplace. It seemed to wriggle and shift and then it began to grow. The boys stared in disbelief. A tiger-skin rug was moving. "It's coming to life," gasped Ed.

The striped body rose upwards to its full size. It shook itself and looked around. The boys froze, as the tiger looked straight at them. The big cat bared huge teeth and let out a terrible roar. The whole room seemed to shake.

The boys shrank backwards and inched slowly along the wall as the tiger, its eyes glinting, followed them. It crouched and got ready to spring. Ed and Matthew waited, frozen with fear.

Suddenly, all the big cats began to move. A black panther hissed and crouched. Lions and a cougar surrounded the boys. There was no way out. The cats came closer and closer. They were stalking their prey.

Ed and Matthew shrank back. They pressed themselves against the wooden panels that lined the walls. Suddenly, there was a slight 'click' and one gave way. The brothers fell backwards, landing with a thud, as the secret wooden door snapped shut behind them. Outside, there was a fierce yowling and scratching. "Where are we?" asked Ed.
"Some sort of secret room," replied Matthew.

The boys looked around. Light filtered through tiny ridges in the wood. In the corner, they saw a wooden tube that was covered in dust. Ed reached over and opened it. Inside was a paper scroll. He unravelled it and began to read. "It says that on each full moon, the animal spirits shall come alive. This is a curse on the Upshire family for years of hunting big cats. The only way to break the curse is for the cats to be outside when the sun rises."

The boys looked at each other. "We've got to tell Lord Upshire," they said together.

The boys carefully opened the secret door. The cats had escaped from the house and were prowling outside. "The boys ran down the long corridors and banged on the bedroom doors, to wake everyone up.

Lord Upshire read the scroll. "It has been lost for years," he said "Now we know how to lift the curse. Come on, everyone, lock all the doors and windows.

Outside, the big cats paced and yowled. The sun was beginning to come up and as it did, each cat gradually began to fade away.

By the time the sun was full in the sky, the cats were gone forever. "Your car will work now," said Lord Upshire to Mr and Mrs Brown. "As for these two brave boys, they will be remembered as the gallant knights who lifted the curse of Upshire Hall."

Matthew and Ed smiled at each other. They couldn't wait to get back home. No one at school was ever going to believe their amazing adventure on the night of the full moon.

# Circus Freaks

Luke was watching the worst circus he had ever seen. He couldn't help yawning. The clowns weren't funny, the acrobats kept falling over and the plate spinner had smashed six plates already. It was a shambles.

Luke's family seemed to be enjoying themselves, but Luke couldn't stand it any more. "I'm going to get some popcorn," he told his brother, as he got up from his seat and wandered outside.

There were no food stalls anywhere. "This is definitely the worst circus I've ever been to," Luke muttered to himself. Then, just as he was about to head back into the big top, he heard a weird noise. Looking behind him, he saw a strange-looking tent. Above the entrance was an old sign made of old, dusty light bulbs that were buzzing and flickering. The sign said, 'POPCORN'.

"Funny how I didn't notice that before," thought Luke. He made his way over to the tent and saw a man appear at the entrance. The man had a big, round stomach and wore a bright red coat. His hair was slicked-back and he had a big, black moustache. The man's eyes were so big, they almost seemed to pop out of his head.

"Welcome," he said, in a loud, ringing voice. "What can I do for you?"
"I'd like some popcorn, please," said Luke, awkwardly.
"I am afraid we are out of popcorn today," said the strange man. "But we do have something else you might enjoy. Would you care to step this way?"
The man stood to the side, to let Luke through.

The tent was gloomy and dim inside. There was something odd about it and Luke was nervous, but he was curious, too. So, he followed the man to a seat in the middle of an empty grandstand.

The man jumped into the central ring, took off his old top hat and bowed. "I am the ringmaster," he announced. "Welcome to the bone-rattling, grave-shaking, foolish, ghoulish, Haunted Circus."

Strange, old-fashioned fairground music began to play. Suddenly, performers entered the ring. There was a lady on stilts, a ghostly lion and clowns riding cockroaches.

Luke was terrified at first, but he couldn't stop watching. The riders made the cockroaches do all kinds of tricks and as a finale, they all took to the air and hovered round each other in a breathtaking dance.

Luke couldn't help clapping. Then, two figures bounded into the ring that were walking, talking skeletons. "Introducing Billy Bones and Sidney Skull," cried the ringmaster. "They're drop dead funny!"

Billy bowed and clattered noisily across to Sidney. "Hey, Sidney," he said, "are you going to the party tonight?"
"No," replied Sidney. "I've got *no body* to go with. Get it?"

The skeleton clowns' routine was brilliant. Sidney stole Billy's skull and wouldn't give it back until Billy started playing the xylophone on Sidney's ribs. By the end, Luke was laughing so hard, he could hardly catch his breath.

The clowns ran off stage and the ringmaster returned. "Now, you will witness the world's finest 'arachnobat'," he said, in a dramatic voice, "meet Spinning Jenny, mistress of the skies."

A spotlight shone high up into the beams of the tent. A gigantic, hairy spider crawled along a rafter. She seemed to bow in Luke's direction and then jumped off the beam. The spider plummeted towards the centre of the ring. "She'll make a terrible mess when she hits the floor," thought Luke, as he watched in horror. But, at the last moment, the huge spider stopped suddenly, suspended on a sliver of silken thread. Then she wiggled her legs and rolled her many eyes, while she spun a delicate web.

"And finally, our star act," boomed the ringmaster, "the lion tamer."

Billy Bones led three, spectral lions out into the ring. The huge animals were ghostly green and massive. They gnashed their teeth and roared.

One of the lions opened its mouth and Billy Bones put his head right in it. The lion's mouth snapped shut over the skeleton's head. But because the lion was ghostly, the skeleton didn't even notice.

When the show was over, the ringmaster held out his hand to Luke. "Won't you join our haunted circus?" he said. "You could stay with us forever." Slowly, all the performers began to beckon to Luke. "Come with us," they said, in a long, slow, hypnotic chant.

Luke's head began to swim with muddled thoughts and he felt sleepy. The performers moved closer towards him, reaching out their hands to him. Suddenly, a great roar of laughter came from the main circus tent.

Luke woke up with a jolt. "I'm sorry," he said. "I don't think I'm cut out for circus life. It's too creepy." All at once, the lights went out and Luke ran as fast as he could, away from the haunted circus.

Back in the big tent, no time had passed. The plate spinner's plates were still wobbling and the audience were shrieking with laughter. Luke sat down by his brother. "Maybe this isn't so bad after all," he thought, "but I definitely won't be joining the circus anytime soon."

# Lair of the Wolfman

It was a sunny day at Monster World Theme Park. Jess, Jake, Ella and Max had just been on the fastest ride ever. "My legs are wobbling," said Ella. "I feel sick," moaned Jess.

Max smiled and looked at Jake. "I think we'd better go on something a bit quieter next," he said and pointed at a big tunnel in the shape of a huge skull. An empty carriage rattled towards the skull's open mouth and stopped near the entrance. "Let's go on the ghost train," said Jake.

The four friends scrambled into the open carriage. The boys jumped into the front, determined to get the best view. "I don't like being at the back," said Jess, "what if we get grabbed?"

The boys just laughed. "It's not real, Jess," said Max, "it's just a bit of fun." Suddenly, the carriage gave a jolt and moved forward into the darkness. Ella looked back to see the sunlit park disappearing behind them.

The tunnel was dark and cold. Nothing moved except the train, which inched forward slowly. "I can't see a thing," said Ella. Her heart pounded. In the pitch black, something hairy brushed past her face. She let out an ear-splitting scream and the boys covered their ears.

A flicker of light revealed cobwebs hanging from the ceiling and a hairy spider that bobbed up and down on a piece of elastic. Rubber bats swooped low and tattered, giant moths dangled from the roof of the tunnel. "It's so fake," said Max, "it's got to be the oldest ride in the park."

The lights began to flicker dimly, as the train track curved into a cave mouth. Above the entrance was a sign that said, *Lair of the Wolfman*. "Oh, no!" cried Jake, in mock horror. "Please, not the Wolfman!"

The train moved into a large chamber that was made to look like a forest. A full moon glowed in the darkness. The sound of distant wolf howls echoed from hidden speakers, as the little train edged further into the cave.

Up ahead, the moonlight pooled around a shadowy figure, crouched near a clump of trees. The body was bent, as if on all fours, yet strangely twisted and hunched. Coarse hair covered the thick, muscular body. The creature's huge head hung low and its blood-shot eyes stared forward, blankly.

The friends stared at the beast. The boys burst out laughing. "It's pathetic," said Jake. However, Jess wasn't laughing and neither was Ella. They didn't think the creature was funny at all. Those vacant, bloodied eyes gave them the creeps. "I want to get out of here," whispered Jess.
"Me, too," said Ella.

The train moved on. Darkness enveloped the carriage and, just as it left the cave, the girls turned to look at the beast. They gasped in horror - its head was turned in their direction and it was looking straight at them.

In the tunnel, the train stopped and the lights went out. The boys clapped their hands. "Fantastic," they said together, expecting some scary fun.

The girls however, were silent. Suddenly, the tunnel began to echo with noises. There was an odd, padding sound, like muffled steps, then a gurgle and a moan. Suddenly, the boys were thrust forward, so much that they almost toppled out of the carriage. A terrible scream rang out, then there was silence. Something laughed and it didn't sound like an animal, or a human. It was savage and chilling.

The lights flickered on. "Wow!" said Jake, looking at Max, "that's more like it. What do you think, girls?" he said, turning round. But the seats behind them were empty. The girls had gone.

"Where are they?" said Max.
"They must have got out," replied Jake, in an anxious voice, "we'll have to get out and look for them."

The boys were beginning to feel uneasy. They got out of the train and walked carefully down the tunnel. The track led back to the lair of the beast. It felt strange and creepy.

Inside the lair, the moon still glowed above the trees, it was unnaturally quiet. There was a scuffling sound from the dark. "What was that?" whispered Jake, clutching Max's arm.
Next, they heard a gasp, then a stifled scream.

In the moonlight, the boys saw the shape of the beast. His head tilted back and he let out a long, slow howl. It was the howl of a hunter with its prey. Jess and Ella were huddled nearby, terrified.

Suddenly, the light of the full moon began to dim. It seemed to make the Wolfman weak. He sank to his knees, howling in pain. Jake seized the opportunity, he darted forward and grabbed the girls.
"Quick," shouted Max, "run for it!"

The four friends ran through the dim lair. Behind them, the Wolfman howled and gnashed his teeth. He leaped after the four friends, his red eyes flashing.

The Wolfman drew closer and closer until, suddenly, he tripped on the tracks. He collapsed on the ground, hunched and moaning. "Keep running," shouted Jess, "don't look back."

The four friends ran for their lives, back down the empty tunnel and into the sunlight. "Wow!" said Jake, gasping for breath. "Was that real?"
"We're not going back in to find out," said the girls. Max laughed.
"Let's go back on the fast ride," said Ella, "it'll be a breeze after the 'Lair of

# The Grimwort Ghosts

The Grimworts were different from other families. They liked dark dungeons and slimy cellars, where no light ever reached. They liked cobwebs and spiders and things that go bump in the night, because the Grimworts weren't ordinary people, they were ghosts.

In an ancient tower, in the middle of a very old city, the Grimworts happily haunted the draughty stairwells and creepy corridors. They loved nothing more than to scare the socks off any visitors who came to call. They especially liked frightening children, because they seemed to scream longer and louder than adults. In fact, the louder the children screamed, the funnier the Grimworts found it. All day long, they lurked silently in the shadows, waiting for their next victim to pass by.

However, the mischievous ghost family had a problem. Egor, the youngest ghost wasn't very good at frightening people. He just couldn't get the hang of it. His parents were very worried. "Do a blood-curdling scream," said Lord Grimwort, one day. So, Egor opened his mouth, as wide as he could, but for some reason, the tiniest, squeakiest, "Oooooooh," sound came out.

Lord and Lady Grimwort looked at each other in a very worried fashion. "Really, Egor," said his mother, "what is the point of being a ghost if you can't scare people?"

Lord Grimwort stood up. A really good, blood-curdling scream sounds like this," he said, opening his mouth so wide, you could see what he'd eaten for breakfast three hundred years ago, when he was still alive.
"AAAARGH!" he screamed. The rats in the dungeon ran for cover and the bats dropped from the ceiling. Egor put his fingers in his ears. His father's screams were really deafening.

"I can rattle my chains," said Egor, "they're scary." He gave his chains a good shake, but they just sounded like a baby shaking its rattle.
"Oh, dear," said Lady Grimwort, disappearing through the dungeon wall. "Whatever are we to do with you, Egor?"

Lord Grimwort looked at the clock. "Some children are coming to see the dungeons this afternoon. Let's give them the fright of their lives," he said, with a dastardly cackle.

Everyone got ready for the haunting. Egor's brother, Oswald, slipped into his costume with bloodstains down the front. "I like scaring children," he cackled. Edmund put on a black hood with slits for eyes. He picked up his executioner's axe, swung it high in the air and waved it around.
"Come on," said Lord Grimwort, "it's time to get to our places."

Lady Grimwort put on her 'lady about to be beheaded' costume, practiced one of her spine-chilling wails and the whole family moved off in the direction of the dungeons.

The dungeons were dark and dank, and eerie shadows slunk in corners. Lord Grimwort suddenly pointed at a rotting, old, empty barrel. "This is what I want you do, Egor," he said. "I want you to hide in this big wooden barrel and when the children come in, I want you to pop your head up and give them a nasty fright."

Egor's father lifted him into the barrel. "Where will you be?" Egor asked. "We're going to terrify the tour guides further down the passage," said Lord Grimwort with a happy smile.
Lady Grimwort kissed Egor. "Be my spookiest son, darling," she said.

Egor settled down and waited. It was comfy in the barrel, but a little too warm for Egor. He liked things nice and chilly. After a few minutes, Egor's eyes started to close. He was almost asleep when he heard noises. "Ugh, this is horrid," said a girl's voice.

"It's creepy," said another voice. "Imagine being imprisoned down here."

"What are those rings on the wall for?" asked a boy with glasses.

"Prisoners were chained there, long ago, and then left to rot," said the teacher. The children looked around. The dungeon was sinister and they didn't like the way it made shivers run down their spines.

Inside the barrel, Egor stood up behind the classmates. He blew his cold, ghostly breath over them. The children felt the hairs standing up on their arms and the backs of their necks, but they didn't know why.

Egor slunk down into the barrel and then jumped up, suddenly. "Whoo!" he wailed and ducked down again. Everyone turned to look.
"Was that you, Adrian?" asked the teacher, looking at a boy with spiky hair.
"No, Miss Jones," said Adrian, glancing nervously around.

Egor rose up again. "Whoo!" he moaned, right in front of the children. Their mouths fell open and their eyes nearly popped out of their heads. Adrian's spiky hair stood up so high, he looked like a hedgehog. The children all screamed at once.

Egor was so surprised, he fell back inside the barrel and banged his chin. "Oooh," he cried, with a long, mournful moan, "Ooooooh!"
The sound echoed in the barrel and seemed to move all around the dark, dank dungeon.

The children were rigid with fright. Then suddenly, they started screaming again and made a mad dash for the door. "Wait," called the teacher, nervously, beginning to run after them. They didn't stop running until they were outside in the warm sunshine.

Egor's family listened with glee from further down the passage. "What terrifying screams," said Lord Grimwort, "how marvellous."

Lady Grimwort put a big bandage on Egor's sore chin and got his favourite tin whistle for him to play. "I think I'm getting the hang of being a proper ghost," he said. "I'm looking forward to haunting tonight."

After that, visitors to the old tower were more scared than ever. They said that they felt cold breaths of air that sent shivers down their spines and heard eerie noises coming from the dungeons. Little did they know that, at last, Egor really had become a Grimwort ghost.

# Tunnel of Terror

One cold evening, Mark and his friends, Joel and Dax, were travelling home from school on the underground. The train was just beginning to slow, on its approach to the next station, when something caught Mark's eye. A shape was moving in the tunnel. "Did you see that?" said Mark, "there's something out there, in the tunnel."

The boys didn't take any notice. "Yeah, right," said Joel, without even looking up from his game console. "Everyone knows that you're always seeing monsters where there aren't any."

But Mark knew he had seen something, slithering along, in the dark tunnel. It had a long, worm-like body, with lots of legs. Mark was determined to find out what it was. "I'm going after it," he said.

"Suit yourself," laughed Joel, "we've got to change trains anyway because they're doing repairs at this station." Just as he spoke, the train slowed to a halt at the platform.

As the last passengers made their way to the exit, Mark hid in a shadowy recess. He listened while the workers set up their equipment for the station repairs. When they eventually went for their evening break, Mark grabbed one of their torches.

Suddenly, the platform was empty and eerily silent. Mark jumped onto the track and set off down the tunnel. It was dark and the small torch didn't light up much of the inky blackness. Mark thought he could hear something slithering towards him in the distance, but when he shone the torch, nothing was there.

Mark scanned the arched tunnel and found streaks of sticky, green slime glowing on the floor and walls. He followed the trail to a huge crack in the floor. As Mark peered into the crack, he could make out what looked like a tangle of shapes, writhing in the weak beam of light.

Suddenly, a noise came from the darkness behind him. Mark clicked off the torch, crept slowly forwards and was swallowed by the dense blackness. A foul stench filled his nostrils, Mark could sense that something was close by. He flicked on the torch and the pale light played over the shiny amber skin of something that appeared to be an enormous, sleeping, centipede.

Without thinking, Mark pulled out his camera from his pocket and took a picture. The camera flash was an explosion of light in the darkness. The startled creature reared up, its limbs waving chaotically, high above Mark's head. Huge, bulbous eyes glowed, like pale orbs. The thing let out a horrible, high-pitched screech. "Oh, no," said Mark in a panic, "that was a big mistake."

The creature began to uncoil its body. Mark turned and fled along the dark tunnel, back towards the station. Behind him, the monster began to move, it's multiple legs scuttling along the old train track.

Mark ran blindly onwards through the tunnel, which seemed endless. He ran until he felt his legs go weak. Suddenly Mark stumbled and fell. The walls echoed the terrifying clatter and rattle of scaly legs that were coming closer and closer.

Mark's blood ran cold, as he turned to see the wriggling underbelly of the gigantic beast rearing up in front of him. "I'm dead," he thought. The torch wasn't bright enough to deter it. Then he remembered the camera.

Quickly, Mark took a picture. The flash momentarily blinded the creature and it shrank back, squealing, allowing him to scramble away.

With shaking hands, the terrified boy shone the torch in front of him. The empty station was just visible up ahead. Heaving himself onto the platform, Mark stumbled and almost fell as he staggered up the motionless escalator.

"I should be safe, now," he thought, his mind racing. "I'll go and find the workmen." But then a scuttling sound echoed off the walls. The giant bug was right behind him. "I can't let it get to the surface," thought Mark. He was almost at the top of the escalator when he had an idea.

The central panel between the escalators made a perfect slide and Mark jumped onto it. There was no time to lose. He could not let the creature get into the outside world. "I must lead the bug back down to that crack in the ground," said Mark, as he slid past the angry creature, waving his torch. The huge bug snaked its long body back round and chased its prey down into the tunnels.

Mark stumbled in the dark and managed to find the crack in the ground. The lumbering creature was right behind him, as Mark jumped across the huge crack and dropped the torch into the blackness.

The giant centipede, drawn by the moving light, followed it and tumbled downwards. Its massive tail lashed wildly and dislodged the loosened brick and rubble, which crashed down, blocking the hole. Mark heard a distant hiss and squeal that, eventually, faded to silence.

Mark couldn't believe what had happened. "Just wait until my friends see my photo," he thought. He felt for his camera, but it had fallen out of his pocket. "Oh well," he sighed, "I may not have proof, but at least I know that monsters really do exist in the 'tunnel of terror'." With that, Mark smiled and made his way up to the surface and to safety.

# The House of Ghosts

Number thirteen, Green Street, was a house where nobody wanted to live. Dan, Megan and Will walked past it on their way home from school everyday. They didn't like the crumbling walls, or the grey, broken windows that seemed to stare at them, like blank eyes. The derelict old house gave them the creeps and they always walked past it quickly.

One afternoon however, something made the three friends stop. In a window, at the top of the house, stood a boy. "Who's that?" asked Megan. Suddenly, the boy began to move. He waved his arms and seemed to be shouting something, although there was no sound.

"What's he saying?" asked Will. "He's saying, 'help me'," replied Megan, peering intently at the figure in the window. Then she gasped. "I know that boy," she said, "it's Charlie Riggs. I think he's in trouble."

Without a word, Will bounded up the steps and banged on the door. It opened with a loud creak, but nobody was on the other side. Will beckoned to the others. "Come on," he said, "we've got to help Charlie."

Megan and Dan followed Will into the house and found themselves in a dark, dusty hallway. The walls were damp and crumbling and strange pictures hung on the walls.

Suddenly, the front door slammed shut behind them. The friends tried to open it but the door was locked. "We're trapped," said Megan. There was a shuffling noise in the hallway behind them. They turned to see a figure, standing at the bottom of the stairs.

An old man had appeared, as if from nowhere. He was strangely dressed and looked unnaturally pale. "So, you've come to rescue the boy?" he asked. The old man wrung his hands and gave a sinister smile. "My house is full of secrets," he cackled, "I warn you to beware." And with that, he disappeared.

Will, Megan and Dan stood frozen to the spot. "Ghost," said Megan, in a small, frightened voice, as she stared at the place where the man had stood.

Will's voice cut through the quiet. "Ghost or not," he said, his voice shaking slightly, "we've got to rescue Charlie. Come on." Will charged towards the stairs and the others followed, scared to be left alone in the hallway.

At the top of the stairs was a doorway to a dimly-lit room. Inside, red-eyed ghouls hovered and hissed as the friends approached. "Go back," they moaned, "you'll never find your friend, he's ours now."

"Ignore them," said Will bravely, "they can't hurt us." He took a deep breath and walked right through the ghostly apparitions, as if they were mist.

Dan and Megan stepped forward to follow Will. Suddenly, a pool of slime appeared on the floor beneath their feet. Megan jumped back, but Dan was too slow, he gave a loud cry as he disappeared into the slime and down a hidden chute. "Dan," called Megan, "can you hear me?"

"I'm fine," said Dan, peering around the dank space where he had landed. "I think I'm in the basement. You carry on, I'll catch you up." Ghostly shapes began to gather around him. They seemed to be sucking the energy from him and Dan was struggling to breathe. Suddenly, a shaft of sunlight shone through a broken shutter. The ghosts wailed and moaned and shrunk backwards. "They don't like the light," said Dan, "I must find the others and tell them."

Near the top of the house, Will and Megan stumbled up a long flight of stairs. "We're nearly there," said Megan, "the attic is on the next floor." But, just as she reached the top step, the stairs transformed into a smooth surface. Will slipped and began to slide downwards. "Hang on!" cried Megan. She grabbed Will's hand and heaved him back up.

"You'll never make it," said a sinister voice. It was a strange ghoul, like a talking head, poking through the bannister.
"Run!" said Will. The two friends scrambled up towards the attic, but the ghosts in the house would not let them through the door. "They're too powerful," said Will, "we'll never open the door."

Suddenly, there was a loud shout behind them. Dan was running up the stairs. He quicky tore open the curtains at the window and let bright sunlight flood in. With terrifying howls and moans, all of the ghosts in the house suddenly disappeared.

In the little attic room, Charlie Riggs watched as the friends burst through the door. "Did the ghosts frighten you?" asked Megan. Charlie just looked at her in a puzzled way.

"Ghosts? There's no such thing," he laughed, "I came up here to explore and the attic door slammed behind me. The lock was jammed, that's all."

Will, Dan and Megan looked at each other and smiled. Everything was quiet now at number thirteen, Green Street. They may not be able to convince Charlie Riggs that he had been held captive by spirits, but they knew the real truth about the house of ghosts.

# Vampire Storm

It was a grey and rainy evening. Dean and Jenna sat by the small desk in Dean's bedroom. "We've got to think of an idea for the school art competition," said Jenna. "Are you listening, Dean?" It was quite obvious that her brother wasn't. He stared intently out of the window, deep in thought.

Outside, street lamps flickered into life. The day was fading and a cold moon had begun to rise. "I know," said Dean, suddenly, making Jenna jump. "Let's do something scary, like a mutant, cyber-vampire. I'll sketch it and you can finish it on the computer."
Jenna smiled. She could always trust her brother's bright ideas.

After much scribbling and rubbing-out, the sketch was ready. Dean had drawn a thin figure with a stooped body and an overly large head. On its face, one eye slanted downwards and the wide mouth sagged in a strange grimace that exposed two sharp, white fangs. Grey eye-bags hung low over hollow cheeks and the picture had all the appearance of a tired undertaker.

Jenna scanned the drawing, then she added light and shadow and a dash of red. "That's brought him to life," said Dean.

Suddenly, something banged hard against the bedroom window. They both jumped back in alarm. "It's just the wind," said Dean. "It's really picking up, there'll be storm tonight, for sure."
Jenna stretched and yawned. "I'm off to bed," she said.

Dean reached over to switch the computer off. "Goodnight creepy vampire," he said. Outside, a bolt of lightning ripped across the sky. The screen buzzed and crackled. Dean pressed the button to shut down, but nothing happened. So, he sloped off to bed, leaving the computer cursor blinking in the dark.

Night crept on. Outside, lightning split the dark. The computer flickered wildly and a pale, green light began to seep from the screen. It spilled out over the desk and down onto the carpet, while outside, thunder crashed and boomed.

Dean woke with a start to see something moving nearby. A familiar figure stood by the window. It was tall with a stooped body and large head. Dean rubbed his eyes and stared in disbelief. The vampire had come alive. "What do you want?" stammered Dean, his heart pounding in his chest.

The figure opened its mouth and said, "Food." Dean flicked on the light. "He's a vampire and he wants food, that means he wants blood!" he cried.

The figure stretched out its arms and moved forward. Frozen with fear, Dean closed his eyes and waited for the first bite, but nothing happened. Instead, there was an odd whooshing noise nearby. When he opened his eyes, he saw that the vampire was draining his bedside lamp of power. The light fizzled, spluttered and then went out.

Dean bolted to Jenna's room and switched on the light. "Get up," he said in a hard whisper, "it's come to life."
"What has?" asked Jenna, sleepily. Then she saw it standing in the doorway. Jenna stifled a scream when the lights went out.
"He's draining the power," said Dean. "He wants the electricity."

The vampire turned around and lumbered towards the stairs. "There's loads of electrical stuff downstairs," croaked Dean.
"Yeah, there's the cooker, the fridge and the brand new TV," said Jenna.
They raced after the creature, trying not to make any noise, in case they woke Mum and Dad up.

Downstairs, the vampire crouched near the fridge. There was a, now familiar, 'whooshing' sound and the fridge stopped humming. "Do something," said Jenna, "if we don't stop him, he'll drain the whole house, maybe even the whole neighbourhood!"

Dean looked around. In a panic, he ran to the sink. He grabbed a jug, half-full of water and threw it over the creature. It made a sloshing, splattering kind of sound. There was a short silence, while the confused figure swayed backwards and forwards, as small sparks flew from its body. Suddenly the creature let out a long moan and fell backwards, with a crash, onto the hall table.

For a moment, the hallway was deathly quiet. Then, a light flicked on upstairs. "What's going on down there?" said an irritated, sleepy voice. It was Dad. The vampire quickly recovered from his dousing when he noticed the light. "Food," it groaned and lurched towards the stairs.

"We've got to distract him," said Dean desperately.
Outside, a stark bolt of lightning flashed. It lit up the hallway. The vampire turned towards it and Dean had an idea. He fumbled for something in the pocket of a coat, hanging in the hallway. Pulling out a bunch of keys, he shoved one in the door lock and opened it with a click.

"Come, on, Vampy," he called, "this way." He flung the door open, just as another bolt of lightning struck. The vampire stumbled out of the door and into the garden. Lightning flashed and thunder boomed. The lashing rain splashed and fizzled on the creature's body. Jenna and Dean watched as it began to judder and fade until nothing was left but a series of small, sputtering sparks.

Dean turned to Jenna. They looked round at the splintered table and then at the strangely quiet fridge in the kitchen. "Dad'll be down the stairs any minute. He'll want an explanation," said Dean.
"We'll put it all down to the storm," said Jenna, "and as for the school art competition, I think we should stick to still life."

# The Haunted Halloween

Everything was ready for Alex's Halloween party. The spooky decorations were hung up, the eyeball sweets were in bowls and the pumpkin cakes were baked. All Alex had to do was put on his Frankenstein's monster costume. He was quite looking forward to having a bolt through his neck.

As the guests arrived, Alex's mum showed them in. Alex put some creepy music on the stereo, full of weird screams and howls. Alex's mum brought out trays of cookies shaped like rats and a whole heap of spider-shaped jellies.

Everyone wore weird and wonderful Halloween costumes. However, Alex noticed three children, standing by the food table. One was dressed as a vampire, another as a skeleton in a cape and the third was a ghost in a sheet. There was something strange about their costumes and Alex went to take a closer look.

The vampire had red eyes that looked real. Underneath the skeleton's cape, its bones didn't seem to have anything holding them up. Then Alex looked at the ghost and he could see right through it!

When nobody was looking, Alex walked right up to the ghost and tugged off its sheet. There was nothing underneath. Alex could hardly speak with surprise. "Excuse me," said a little voice, in the space where a body should have been. "Please replace my sheet, I feel invisible without it."
"But you are invisible," whispered Alex, his mouth open wide.

Alex quickly replaced the sheet before anyone noticed. "Please don't be angry with us," said the skeleton, its bones clacking noisily. "We are friendly spooks, honestly."

"My name is Vertebra," said the skeleton. "The vampire is Vlad and our ghostly friend is Jasper. We came to your party because no one on Hallows End Road, where we live, wants to celebrate Halloween. They all think it's boring."

Alex felt sorry for his new spooky friends. He was sure that, with a little encouragement, their neighbours would join in the Halloween celebrations. Then he had an idea. "My party is nearly over," he said. "Everyone will be going off trick or treating, why don't we go to Hallows End Road?"

"I'm coming with you," insisted Alex's mum, when he told her. "Where is this place, anyway?" she asked, "I've never heard of it."

Hallows End Road was much nearer to Alex's house then he, or his mum, realised. "I can't imagine why we have never noticed it before," said Mum. She looked around at the misshapen houses that lurked in shadow, under the bright, full moon and she felt strangely uneasy.

It was getting dark when Alex knocked at the door of a ramshackle house. The front door creaked open and a man with a hairy, wolf-like face and clawed hands, stood grinning at them. "Trick or treat," said Alex bravely.
The man growled, threw some cookies at them and slammed the door.

"How rude," said Alex's mum, "but I have to say, that Wolfman costume looked incredibly real." She laughed nervously and the others just looked at each other.

Vertebra examined one of the cookies. "They're dog biscuits," she said, throwing them into a flower bed. "What a nasty trick."

The second house was as big as a castle. It was opened by a hunchbacked man with huge, bulging eyes. "Do you wish to speak to the master?" he said in a creepy, whispery voice.

"Actually, we wanted to know if you'd like a trick or a treat," replied Alex.

Before the hunchback had time to answer, a scary voice boomed out from the grim hall behind. "At last, I have almost brought the monster to life," shrieked the mad voice. There followed a terrible crackling sound and a hideous groaning and moaning.

The hunchback looked frightened. "We must not anger the master," he said and quietly closed the door.

Next, Alex knocked on the door of a horrible cottage. It was opened by a ragged-looking witch. She had long, filthy nails and limp, greasy hair. There was a suspicious sound of bubbling coming from inside the cottage and a terrible smell wafted past.

The witch smiled and cackled, loudly. "Here you go, children," she wheezed, handing them some very weird-looking, black sweets. "This is my finest recipe, black beetles in castor oil. Try them, they're delicious." With that, the witch gave an ear-piercing shriek and shut the door.

Vlad tasted one of the sticky sweets and promptly spat it out. "It tried to bite me back," he said.
"I think I've had enough of Halloween," said Vertebra, "I want to go home."

She led them to a tall house at the end of the road and knocked on the door. A skeleton appeared, wearing clothes like tramp. "Dad!" cried Vertebra. She ran into the house and hugged the skeleton with a clackety, rattling sound. Vlad and Jasper followed her inside.

Alex's Mum went rather pale. "There is something very strange about the people who live around here," she whispered, "I think I'd like to go home, too." Alex, quickly lead his bewildered mother down the garden path.

"Please come and visit us again," pleaded Vertebra.
"Goodbye, Alex," said Vlad and Jasper, "we hope we didn't ruin your party?"
"No," said Alex, "you made this the best haunted Halloween ever."

# The Black Tower

Callum stared out of the window. He couldn't believe his eyes. "Mum!" he shouted, "come and look at this." In the distance, on the edge of town, a huge, black tower had appeared from nowhere. The tower was unlike anything Callum had ever seen before. It had smooth, curved sides, with narrow windows and a spiky, pointed top. It was such a deep black that it seemed to swallow up light. It was the most mysterious and exciting thing Callum had ever seen.

"Where did it come from?" Callum asked his mother.
"I don't know," she replied, "but there's something unnatural about it. That tower is sinister and I don't want you to go anywhere near it."

Callum wasn't listening, he was thinking about how long it would take for him to get to Holly and Beth's house, so that they could go and see the black tower close up.

A short time later, the three friends approached the silent, imposing tower. "It looks like the kind of place a vampire would live," said Beth.

Suddenly, there was a hissing sound nearby. A fleeting shadow disappeared down a flight of strange-looking steps that had emerged from the side of the tower. Cautiously, the friends crept towards the steps and could not resist climbing up them to see inside the tower.

Callum led the way into a gloomy corridor, where arched walls moved in and out as if they were breathing the hot, sticky air. Strange, bulbous lamps lined the walkway and gave off a low shimmering light that pulsed with a hypnotic, humming noise.

"I don't like it here," whispered Beth, "let's go back." But Callum and Holly continued slowly along the corridor, looking at the smooth, clammy walls that breathed like some strange, living skin.

Suddenly, Beth saw a shadow and heard a muffled padding sound from the corridor up ahead. She pushed Callum and Holly into an alcove and they held their breath at the sight of what was approaching.

It was a tall, yellowish creature with frilled lobes of skin around its mouth and big, bulging, frog-like eyes. It had two splayed toes and huge hands. A thick, putrid waft of air made them wince as the creature passed by without noticing them. "Yuck, what was that?" said Holly, "it's so ugly and it stinks."

"I think it's an alien," said Callum in a worried voice, "let's follow it, we have to find out if there are more of these things, otherwise the whole town could be in very grave danger."

The friends followed cautiously and found themselves on a balcony above a large, circular room, lit by more of the strange, pulsing lights. Below, the creature from the corridor joined three others, who surrounded, what looked like, an ordinary dog.

"We have captured an earth animal," said one of the creatures, in a weird, bubbling voice that sounded like it was speaking and gargling water at the same time.

"Commence the experiment," said another.

The creatures stared at the dog and the humming sound grew louder and louder until it was deafening. Suddenly, the dog began to float upwards.

"It is a success!" exclaimed one of the creatures. "If we can control animal matter, we can control human matter, too. Soon they shall be our slaves."

At that moment, Beth let out a squeal of fear. The creatures jerked their heads to look up. "Human subjects!" they cried. "We must capture them before they alert other earth beings." The aliens fixed their gazes on the three friends, who could feel their bodies beginning to float upwards.

Suddenly, the little dog, who had been barking furiously, bit one of the creatures and it fell back onto a control panel. There was a deep rumble and the sound of massive engines firing. "Oh, no," said Callum, "this isn't a tower, it's a spaceship and it's about to take off. Run!"

Holly, Beth and Callum reached down, grabbed the frightened dog and ran for their lives.

 78

The tower began to shake, as if it was about to break apart. The friends bounded along the dim corridors that were now hot and stinking. They flung themselves down the steps on the outside of the tower, just as they were retracting into the side of the spaceship.

The black tower began to move. Huge flames emerged from its base and then, suddenly, it shot into the sky with a massive whoosh, leaving nothing but a blackened hole behind it.

"Wow," said Callum, "Mum will never believe this." The dog barked and licked Callum's face. Everyone laughed. There had been enough adventure for one day, but at least they had solved the secret of the black tower.

# The Phantom

Mr Pratchett was getting impatient. "Hurry up, boys," he shouted. "The light's fading and we don't want to set up camp in the dark." It was Summerhill High's annual trip to the wilderness and things weren't going well. The school bus driver had already fixed a flat tyre and now they were lost.

There was a lot of noisy laughter from the group of boys in the bus. Joe, Billy and Alex looked out of the back window. Miss Meeks, their teacher, was asking a bewildered, red-faced man for directions. The man was pointing somewhere in the distance and looked concerned.

The bus juddered into life. Miss Meeks jumped on board and slumped into the seat next to Mr Pratchett. "Honestly," she said, "all I wanted were directions to the campsite. That man went on and on about some figure that roams the moors, a phantom or something. I've never heard anything so ridiculous. Anyway, there's a left hand turn somewhere up the road. It's easy to miss, so we'll have to be careful."

The bus pulled off with a slow rumble. Billy and Joe had heard Miss Meeks talking. "A phantom on the moor," said Billy, "this could be an interesting trip." The boys looked out of the back window. The red-faced man stood with his arms crossed, shaking his head. The sun was sinking and a faint veil of mist had slunk slowly down the mountainside.

It was dark by the time Mr Pratchett realised that they were lost again. The boys tried to stifle their laughter. They loved it when teachers messed up. "We'll have to camp on the moor tonight," said Mr Pratchett, with a sigh. "Come on, you lot, follow me."

Billy, Joe and Alex grabbed their stuff and joined the line of boys following their teacher's torchlight. After a while, Alex hung back, "I think I've dropped my compass," he said, "I won't be a minute." Miss Meeks told him to hurry up.

After much scrabbling and clanking of poles, the camp was complete. Billy hammered in the last tent peg. Then he heard the noise. It was like a long, drawn-out moan from somewhere in the distance. A sudden waft of cold air made him shiver. "Where's Alex?" he said. Joe shrugged his shoulders. They searched around the campsite. Alex was not there.

It fell to Mr Pratchett to search for the missing boy. He set off into the dark, calling Alex's name. Billy thought he saw a shaft of light moving nearby. He called out, but no-one answered. "Must be the wind," he said to Joe.

The boys climbed into their tents and zipped up the flapping canvas. In the distance, they could here Mr Pratchett calling out. Billy felt a nagging feeling in his stomach. Suddenly there was a loud cry on the moor.

Everyone scrambled out of their tents. "What was that?" said a scared voice. Miss Meeks pushed into the group of boys holding torches. "Quiet boys," she said, "I'm going to look for Alex and Mr Pratchett. Stay here and don't move."

Miss Meeks set off, alone, into the black night and most of the boys went back to bed. Billy and Joe remained, feeling anxious.

The wind curled and snaked around the camp, rattling pans and rustling canvas. A strange moaning echoed and Billy was sure he saw the silhouette of a woman watching them. "Is that you, Miss Meeks?" he said. But no one answered.

Suddenly, a terrible scream came from the moor. There was a flurry of movement as the other boys scrambled back to the centre of the camp.
"This is creepy," said one nervous boy.
"Ssssh," said Joe, "let's listen."
A hulking figure was moving in the darkness. From its centre, a small light winked on and off, like a glittering eye. It squelched and groaned, then it let out a series of short gasps and grunts. "It's the phantom," stuttered Billy, "it's real."

Each boy shone a torch towards the thing from the moor. It had three sets of eyes and it was the ugliest thing they had ever seen. They stared as it lurched closer and closer, until the creature was nearly in the camp.

Suddenly, the beast spoke, "Stop shining that light in my eyes!"
It was Mr Pratchett and he wasn't happy. In fact, he was in a foul mood.
He hobbled into the camp, covered from head to toe in mud. Clinging to him was Miss Meeks and on the end was Alex.

Later, Alex explained how he had got lost looking for his compass. "Mr Pratchett dropped his torch and fell into a swampy marsh," he said. "When Miss Meeks stumbled on him in the dark, she thought she'd found the phantom!"

At last, Billy and Joe settled down to sleep. Just as he was drifting off, Billy was sure he heard the sound of a voice calling from the moor. "Must be the phantom," he whispered and fell into a deep sleep.

# Blood Spider

It was the evening before school sports day. Ben wasn't looking forward to it. He always came last in the races, thanks to his asthma. It didn't help that Roy Briggs, the fastest runner in the school, laughed at Ben when he was practicing.

"I wish I was stronger and able to run faster," said Ben, as he gasped for breath. He sat at the edge of the sports field and fumbled for his inhaler, but it slipped from his hand and dropped into the long grass. As Ben reached down, a sharp pain shot through his hand.

"Ouch!" cried Ben, sucking his finger, which was throbbing painfully. It was then that he noticed the spider. It was small with a blood-red stripe across its back, it was unlike any species he had ever seen. It scuttled off into the grass before Ben could capture it.

Back in class, the afternoon dragged. Ben forgot about the small bite on his hand until it began to throb again, later in the day. When he looked at it, two small puncture marks were visible and he noticed that the veins around the wound had swollen and ran like thick, purple rivulets towards his fingers. The throbbing in Ben's hand seemed to get worse. It was as if it was spreading slowly, making its way around his body. Ben was worried. "I've got to find out what kind of spider bit me," he thought. "I'll go and see Alice, she'll be able to help."

The school bell rang and Ben dashed outside. He headed towards Alice's house, jogging slowly at first and then going faster and faster, blood pumping furiously through his veins. The roads and traffic seemed like a blur and suddenly, he was standing outside Alice's front door.

Alice, Ben's best friend looked in every book she could think of, but there was no such spider anywhere. The only book left was one belonging to her Dad, about myths and legends. Alice scanned it and suddenly let out a surprised gasp. "According to this, you have been bitten by a blood spider," she said. "They are the stuff of legend. Anyone bitten by this spider can move extremely fast and they're almost unstoppable."

It was getting late. "I've got to go," said Ben. Alice agreed to do some research on the mythical spider and let him know what she found. Meanwhile, Ben raced home at the speed of light.

Ben went to bed and didn't speak to anyone. His hand was throbbing and even his bones seemed to hurt. He looked down and saw that his hands were pulsing and thick, long nails were growing. "What's happening to me?" asked Ben, as a cold rush of fear swept over him. He switched off the light and dived under the covers. Eventually the wild pulsing lessened and he fell into an uneasy sleep.

The next day was sports day. Ben felt quite normal as he got changed in the locker room. Then, suddenly, a fly buzzed past. He had to resist a powerful urge to snatch at the fly and stuff it into his mouth. Luckily, the teacher had just called the class outside, the first race was about to begin and Ben was running in it.

On the track, everyone lined up for the race. Roy threw his usual sneering looks at Ben. Then, the starting whistle blew. Ben could feel the spider venom rushing through him. He let Roy take the lead, but, just as the finish line was in sight, Ben shot forward in a burst of spider-speed. Roy was astonished to see him hurtle past and win the gold medal.

After the race, Alice ran up to him. "I did some more research," she panted. "The spider venom only stays in the body until the full moon and that's tonight. However, the symptoms might get worse, before they get better," she warned.

Ben was just relieved that he wasn't going to be a spider-freak forever. He changed into his normal clothes and smiled at the thought of Roy's fury at losing the race. Then Ben looked in the mirror and his blood ran cold.

His eyes had turned bright red. "I hope Alice is right about this wearing off by tonight," he said, suddenly worried. Ben pulled his sweatshirt hood over his head and made his way home, hoping he wouldn't see anyone.

Walking down the last street that led to his house, Ben heard someone coming up behind him. Without warning, he was shoved roughly into a shadowy area under a clump of trees. Then a familiar voice spoke. "Hey, freak," hissed Roy Briggs, "how did you win that race? No one can run faster than me."

Ben felt the venom tingle as it rushed through his veins. "But I did run faster," he said, "so, you'd better watch out."

Roy looked Ben up and down and burst out laughing. "I'm not scared of a weakling like you," he said, maliciously.

Ben stepped out of the shadows and pushed the hood back, off his head.
His eyes blazed red and he bared a mouth full of sharp, pointed teeth.
Roy stared with a rigid mask of horror fixed on his face. Then, he gave a
high-pitched squeal and ran away as fast as he could.

That night, the full moon shone brightly. The venom seemed to drain from
Ben's body. His eyes lost their red tinge and his teeth became blunt again.
"I don't think I'll be having any trouble with Roy Briggs in future," he chuckled
to himself. However, Ben decided that, for now at least, he had no intention of
turning into a blood spider.

# The Stone Horseman

Lee and Ged had almost reached the cave. They were on an adventure holiday with their friends, camping in the middle of a vast rainforest. Everyone else had got tired and gone back to camp, but Lee and Ged wanted more excitement.

The entrance to the cave was matted with cobwebs. "It looks like nobody's been here for a very long time," said Lee. The boys broke through the webs and stepped into a wide, airy cave. A shaft of light shone onto a massive statue of a helmeted man, carrying a huge sword and riding a rearing horse. The statue was made of dark marble, with dark red lines running through it that almost looked like veins.

"It's a bit creepy," said Lee, but Ged interrupted him. "Look at this!" he cried. On a stone plinth, near the statue, was an enormous, glittering, blood-red, jewel. "This will make a great souvenir," said Ged, grabbing the jewel. Suddenly, there was a huge crashing sound and a great cloud of dust whirled round the cave. When it cleared, Lee and Ged saw that the plinth was empty. The stone horseman had gone.

The boys were spooked and stood in silence. Cold shivers ran down their spines. "I don't like it here," stammered Lee. "Me, neither," said Ged, "I think we should leave." The two boys scrambled out into the sunlight and ran back towards the camp. They ran so fast, they didn't notice the giant hoofprints leading off into the forest.

Back at the camp, the boys showed the jewel to their friend, George. "You shouldn't have taken this," he warned, "there are all sorts of legends about this forest." But Lee and Ged were far too frightened to go back to the cave.

That night, just as they were going to sleep, the boys heard a noise outside their tent. It was a low, deep, thundering sound, like giant hooves. Suddenly, the jewel began to glow in the darkness. Ged and Lee were terrified. They lay awake all night, waiting for the stone horseman to ride over them, but after some time, the sounds gradually faded into silence.

The next morning, Lee found hoofprints all around the tent. They were far bigger than any horse he'd ever seen. "It wants the jewel back," said Lee. Ged knew that what he said was true.

That day's activity was a rafting trip down the river. The boys were so busy trying to stay in the boat, they almost forgot about the stone horseman. That was until Ged saw a large, shadowy figure, lurking in a clump of trees along the riverbank. Ged pulled Lee's arm to get his attention, but when they looked round, the figure had gone.

That evening, Lee and Ged were both nervous. George came to see them and they all kept looking out for dark shapes in the trees around the camp.

"I don't like this," said Lee, "we should never have taken that jewel."
As he spoke, the sound of thundering hooves filled the air. The trees shook and the stone horseman burst through.

George and Ged dived to the floor, as the stone horse leaped right over them, landing with a crashing sound. "This way!" yelled Lee, dashing into the bushes.

In the distance, lights came on and they could hear shouts as the camp woke up. George dived into a tent. Ged followed Lee, as he scrambled up a ledge to look down on the camp. Below, the stone horseman charged around and raised its sword, threateningly.

Ged took the glowing jewel out of his pocket. "This is what it wants," he said. Suddenly, the stone horseman noticed the jewel. He galloped straight up the ledge towards the boys. "Run!" cried Ged, "we've got to get this jewel back to the cave.

Lee and Ged clambered to the very top of the rocky incline and scrambled down the other side, into the forest. Behind them, the sound of hooves clattering on rock grew louder. Ged took the jewel out of his pocket. It glowed and seemed to be pulling him in a particular direction. "This must be the way back to the cave," he said. "Come on, let's go."

The boys sprinted through the sweltering forest, guided by the stone. The sounds of tree branches tearing and crashing behind them made them run even faster.

After what seemed like ages, the cave came into sight. The boys were exhausted, but they could hear the thundering of hooves right behind them. The trees were shaking and, in an instant, the stone horesman had burst through the leaves and was galloping at full speed, to get his revenge.

Ged and Lee hurtled into the cave, tripping and stumbling towards the plinth. The whole cave shook as the stone horseman entered. At that moment, Ged placed the jewel back on the plinth.

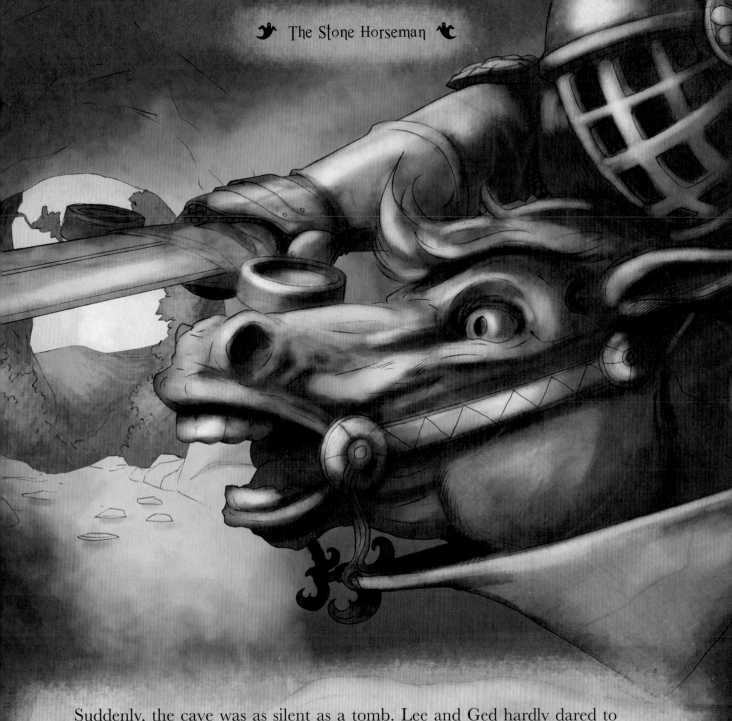

Suddenly, the cave was as silent as a tomb. Lee and Ged hardly dared to look round. When they did, they saw the stone horseman galloping towards them with his sword pointed right at them, but now, he was frozen forever on his plinth.

"Phew," said Lee, "I think we've had enough adventure for one holiday. The next time I want a souvenir, I'm sticking to the gift shop!"

# The Terrible Twins

It was a normal day at school. As usual, Mr Bleak, the strictest teacher in the school, was in a stern mood. He had told the class to be quiet, but he could still hear someone talking. "Is that you, Sykes?" he said to a boy at the back of the classroom.

"It wasn't me, Sir," answered the boy. "It was Albert and Arthur." Mr Bleak looked puzzled and then annoyed. "There are no children called Albert and Arthur in this class, you silly boy."

The rest of the class giggled. "Silence!" shouted Mr Bleak. But there was still talking coming from somewhere in the classroom. Mr Bleak gave a cold, hard look at each pupil and demanded to know who the culprits were.

Everyone turned to look at the back of the classroom. Albert and Arthur were sitting next to each other at a spare table. The whole class could see them clearly, all except Mr Bleak. He simply could not see the two ghosts that were haunting his classroom. Albert and Arthur were two naughty ghosts who loved playing tricks on teachers.

Mr Bleak clapped his hands. "Enough of this childish behaviour," he said. "This morning, we are going to do some algebra."

Some of the children groaned. Mr Bleak picked up a pen. "Now," he said, "I am going to write some sums on the white board and then I'm going to ask you to give me the answers." He turned to the white board and wrote lots of different sums.

Each time someone gave the correct answer, Mr Bleak wrote a harder sum. It took longer and longer to get the answers. The children started looking at the clock. They all wished that the lunchtime bell would ring.

Suddenly, Albert and Arthur left their seats and crept up behind the teacher. They rubbed out the answers to the sums and wrote wrong ones instead. The children laughed and pointed at the white board. When Mr Bleak turned round, he went a funny shade of red. "Who did this?" he shouted.

When the class answered that it was Albert and Arthur, Mr Bleak looked like he was about to explode, "Who are these invisible children," he said, with his teeth clenched, "ghosts?" And then Mr Bleak laughed, as if it was the most ridiculous thing he had ever heard.

But, no sooner had the words left his mouth, when the pens on his desk rose in the air, floated over to the white board and rubbed out everything he had written. Mr Bleak stared with his mouth open and then carried on as if nothing had happened. "Maybe it's time I had a holiday," he thought to himself.

The terrible twins played a prank on Mr Bleak everyday. They nudged his arm when he tried to take the register. They wouldn't let him tidy his desk. As fast as he put things away, they got them out again. They even tied Mr Bleaks shoe laces together, which they found very amusing, indeed.

Mr Bleak didn't know what to make of it. He didn't shout at the children any more because he was too busy waiting for something to happen. In any case, he couldn't blame the children because Mr Bleak never actually saw any of them doing anything. He was beginning to wonder if the children were right. What if there were ghosts in his classroom?

Then, one day, Albert and Arthur were feeling extra mischievous. Mr Bleak was busy tidying books in the classroom, when the naughty twins began to move them around. Mr Bleak couldn't believe his eyes. Next, Albert and Arthur began to moan and howl and wail like ghouls. Mr Bleak was white with fright. Everything in the classroom was moving, all by itself. It was true, the classroom really was haunted.

"Aaaargh!" screamed Mr Bleak, running out into the playground and waving his arms, frantically. He left Albert and Arthur rolling around and giggling, so much they thought they would burst. This was the best fun ever.

"Ahem," said a voice behind the ghost boys. A woman stood in the corner of the room. She wore a long, old-fashioned dress. Her hair was tied neatly in a bun and she wore small, round glasses. "Oh, no," said the twins, looking at each other and then back at the woman. "It's Miss Shiverton." She had been their teacher when they were alive and now she had come back to get them.

The woman spoke. "I warned you," she said, "if you continued to be naughty, I would come back to haunt you. You have played one too many tricks on poor Mr Bleak."

Arthur and Albert looked scared. Mr Bleak was an angel compared to Miss Shiverton. The two naughty ghost twins turned to leap through the door. They just wanted to get away.

"Stay exactly where you are!" said Miss Shiverton, in her sternest voice. She held out a long, spindly cane. The boys froze. "Come with me, you two are in detention. There will be no more pranks in this classroom."
The twins hung their heads and turned obediently to follow their teacher. With that, Arthur, Albert and Miss Shiverton disappeared through the classroom wall.

After that Mr Bleak was always in a good mood and never shouted. But sometimes, when the home time bell had rung and the school was quiet, the corridors echoed with mysterious sounds. Mr Bleak would get shivers down his spine and run to the exit as fast as he could. After all, he never knew when the terrible twins might return.

# The Weird Wishes

Karl and Andy stared at the black, wooden box they had just discovered in Andy's back yard. It was about the size of a shoebox and covered in strange carvings. "It looks weird," said Andy, "don't open it."

Karl ignored his friend and tried to pry the lid off. With a loud crack, the lid flipped open. There was a musty waft of air, then a scaly creature flew out and hovered next to them. The creature looked like a lizard, with bright eyes, purple scales, a yellow belly and a long, swishing tail. It had hands like a monkey's paws, and a big, grinning mouth.

"What is it?" gasped Andy.
To their surprise, the creature answered. "I'm a genie," it said.
"You don't look like a genie," said Karl. "Genies come out of lamps. They wear earrings and pointy shoes."

The creature hissed at the boys. "I am not a genie of fairytales," it said. "You have three wishes. What's your first one?"

Before Andy had a chance to speak, Karl blurted out a wish. "I wish we looked like really cool monsters," he said.
"Your wish is my command!" said the genie.

The genie swished its tail and the boys began to shiver and change. Karl had clawed feet, green hair, orange skin and horns coming out of his forehead. Andy was covered in fur and had big ears and fangs. The friends looked at each other in amazement.

When Andy's little sister saw her brother and his friend, she screamed and ran upstairs. "Monsters!" she cried. Andy and Karl went out into the street to see their friends, but their friends yelled in fright. "Help!" they shrieked. "We're being attacked!"

Everyone on the street stopped and stared at the monster boys. Some people laughed and others screamed. "Get them!" someone cried. "They're monsters!"

"Run!" shouted Andy, and they fled down the street. They heard police sirens and found that they were heading straight towards a parked police car. It screeched to a halt just as they raced down a side street.

The genie was cackling behind the escaping boys. Suddenly, the alleyway turned into a dead end. The policeman chased after them, followed by a big crowd of angry-looking people. "This is horrible," said Karl, "I wish there was a way to fight back!"

"Your wish is my command!" said the genie.

Suddenly, Karl and Andy felt themselves growing. They started to rise above the people, until they were giant-sized. They stepped easily over the brick wall. Karl leaned down towards the crowd and roared, as loud as he could. The people scattered in fear. "That's more like it!" Karl said.
"I'll race you to the top of that tower block over there!" said Andy.

The monster friends easily climbed to the top of the tower block, where they could look over all of the city. They heard a buzzing sound in the distance. It was a swarm of police helicopters, coming to chase them.

Andy tried to swat them as they flew past, but he leaned too far over the edge and lost his balance. "Help!" he cried, as he toppled off the edge of the building.

Karl remembered that he still had a wish. "I wish Andy could fly," he said to the genie. There was a moment of silence and then Andy reappeared, flapping huge bat-wings. The helicopters flew away in fright.

Andy landed and sat next to Karl. "This isn't fun at all," he said. "Everyone hates us and we've used up all of our wishes."

The genie gave a sinister laugh. I like seeing everyone make a mess of their wishes. You've used them up and now you will stay looking like monsters." "Wait," said Andy, "Genie, you granted Karl his three wishes, but what about my three?"

The genie looked annoyed. "Oh, I suppose you can have three, too," he grunted.

"Okay," said Andy, "first, I wish we looked like ourselves again."

Karl and Andy shivered, and found that they were back to their normal size and shape. "Now I wish we were all back in the garden," said Andy. The genie lashed its tail and a fierce wind blew up. It picked them up and whirled them back to Andy's back yard.

"And finally," said Andy, "I wish that you, genie, would return to your box and not come out."

"Nooo!" cried the genie, but it had no choice. With a whoosh, it flitted back into the black box. The lid slammed shut, sealing the genie inside.

"Phew," said Karl, "thanks for using your wishes to save us, Andy."

Andy and Karl buried the box deep in the yard, where nobody would ever find it. Andy switched the portable radio on. "Breaking news," said the announcer, "mystery monsters have run amok in the city!"

"Do you think anyone would believe us if we said those monsters were us?" Karl asked Andy. "We could be famous!"

"You wish!" Andy said, laughing.

# The Mummy's Tomb

Olly lived right next door to a history museum. His dad was the curator and sometimes, after school, Olly would help out and get to see all the strange objects and creepy statues on display.

One evening, Olly's dad was busy translating ancient Egyptian symbols when suddenly, he jumped up. "This is very exciting," he said. "These words are part of an ancient ceremony. I can't quite figure out what they mean, but I'm very close. I need to go down into the basement library and do some research. Can you stay up here and keep an eye on things, Olly? I won't be long."

Olly was excited and nervous, all at the same time. Dad was only going to be downstairs, in the basement, but when Olly heard the distant thunk of the basement door closing, he felt very alone.

The sudden silence seemed to descend like a cold, dense mist. Olly looked around. Behind him, stood the ancient egyptian burial casket that his dad had been studying. Some of his notes were on a stand nearby and Olly couldn't resist taking a look at them.

"Dad must be trying to figure out what the symbols drawn on the casket mean," thought Olly, looking at the writing. He read the title out loud. "Sar-co-ph-a-gus," Olly knew that was the name of the casket. Then he began to read the unfamiliar word below, curious to know what it sounded like, "Mun-ra-nat-sey." The word echoed around the silent room.

Suddenly, there was a dry, creaking noise. Olly turned around to see that slowly, the lid of the sarcophagus was opening. Ancient dust rose in clouds around the casket.

A thin figure stood inside, wrapped tightly in old, brown bandages. As Olly watched, in horror, one of the mummy's arms rose up and pointed at him. Then the creature stepped out of its burial chamber.

Olly stumbled and began to run. Behind him, the mummy followed with jerky, lurching movements. Olly dashed into the next room and scrambled frantically onto a huge statue of a Persian bull's head. He watched as the mummy lurched into the room and turned its bandaged head to look right up at him.

The creature began to climb up the giant statue. Olly could smell the strange odour of the ancient bandages, as the mummy got closer. Somehow, he had to escape. Olly leaped down to the floor and ran. He ran out of the door and down a dark corridor.

"I've got to try and get to the basement," thought Olly. "Dad will know what to do." But the basement door was on the other side of the museum. Olly had gone the wrong way.

The creature was gaining ground and Olly began to panic. He ran into the nearest room and closed the doors behind him.

In the low light, he saw two statues nearby. Using all of his strength, Olly dragged them in front of the door. "That will stop him," he said, panting.

"Not for long," growled a voice, behind him. It was coming from a large stone sphinx on a pedestal. Its eyes glowed like gold. "My master, the pharaoh, is angry," boomed the sphinx. "You should not have spoken the word of power. It has awoken the pharaoh from three thousand years of sleep."

"Oh, I didn't mean to," said Olly, "I'm really sorry, honestly, I help my dad to take care of all the things in the museum. I just wanted to know what the word sounded like when I said it out loud."

The sphinx's eyes glowed. "Please, help me," begged Olly, "tell me, how I can stop the mummy?"
"You must say the word of power in reverse," said the sphinx.

Suddenly, there was a shuffling and groaning sound outside.

The door burst open, toppling the two statues, which crashed to the floor. The mummy lumbered towards Olly, arms outstretched. Olly quickly said the magic words in the reverse order, "Yes-tan-ar-num." The mummy stopped and everything was still.

Then the creature began to unwrap the bandages around its head. Underneath, was the face of a boy, not much older than Olly. "You woke me from my sleep," he said, "Now that you have reversed the word of power, I will sleep again, but before I return to my tomb, I will grant you a wish."

Olly looked around at the broken door and damaged statues. "Please, can you make the museum go back to how it was?" he said.

The pharaoh raised his arms and a great, hot wind whirled around him. The pieces of the broken statues flew together and the smashed doors restored themselves.

The wind pulled the boy paraoh back into his sarcophagus and the lid shut tightly. A deathly silence fell over the museum. Olly couldn't believe what had just happened. Was it all just a dream?

When Dad came back up from the basement, he was very excited. "I think the word on the sarcophagus is part of a ceremony that revives the dead," he said. "I don't really believe it's possible, but it's probably best not to say it anyway." Olly smiled and looked at the mummy's tomb. "Yes, let the pharaoh sleep," he whispered.

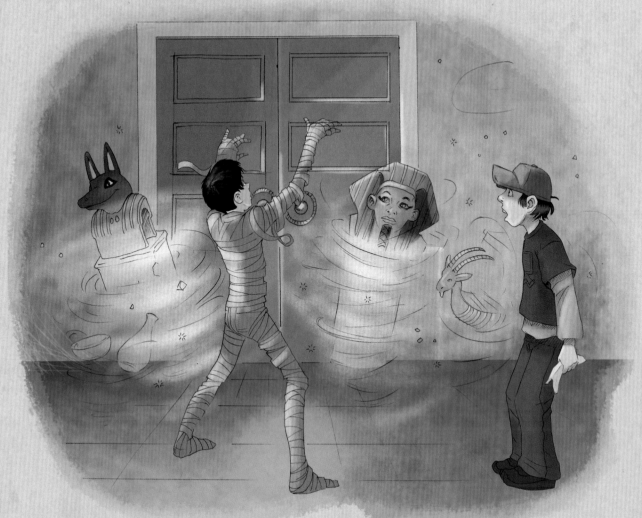

# The Black Dog

Jack was bored. It was bad enough that he'd been packed off to stay with his aunt and uncle, but they lived in the middle of nowhere, on the edge of a huge forest. There was no one here for him to play with and there wasn't even a television.

Uncle Bill warned Jack about the dangers of the forest, such as pits and crags and huge potholes. Aunt Vera kept saying that it was a shame that 'Andy' wasn't there anymore, because he would have kept an eye on him. Jack didn't have a clue who she was talking about.

One afternoon, Jack was well and truly fed up. He was determined to explore the forest. So, while his aunt and uncle were having a nap, he crept through the kitchen and slipped, unseen, out of the back door.

The forest was vast and awesome. Jack had not gone far into it when he noticed that a huge storm was brewing overhead. Dark clouds began to gather and covered the sun. Where the forest had been light, there was now a deep gloom. Jack stumbled forward, finding it hard to see. Suddenly, he slipped and fell, tumbling over and over until he landed with a painful thud.

Jack looked up and saw that he had fallen down a steep slope. The rain drummed down all around him. Soon he was soaked to the skin.

Nearby, a dark shadow moved among the trees. Jack watched as it came closer and closer. The shape seemed to shimmer and glow in the gloom. Jack rubbed his eyes. He thought he must have dust in them.

The shape came closer and closer. It was a black dog with a white patch on its forehead. It sat in front of Jack and panted. "Here, boy," said Jack and held out his hand. The dog came closer and Jack studied it for a while.

The dog seemed friendly, but there was something odd about it. In the light, it seemed to shimmer and shift. Rain fell all around the dog, but did not seem to touch its coat. "I must have banged my head pretty hard," thought Jack.

Suddenly, the dog ran up to the slope and barked, as if it wanted Jack to follow. Even though the animal was big, it didn't dislodge a single pebble. It was as if it didn't weigh anything at all. Jack clambered gingerly upwards, trying not to slide on the stones and small boulders that had been loosened by the rain.

It was a difficult climb. Jack was almost at the top when, suddenly, he slipped. He felt himself start to slide back down and, as he grabbed at rocks and boulders, they dislodged and Jack began to fall. Before he could cry out, Jack felt something pushing him. The dog had run behind Jack and stopped his fall.

Breathing hard, Jack began to climb again, inching his way to the top of the slope. He gave one last, final pull and stood up. But this was not the part of the forest where he had fallen. "I must have climbed up a different way," he said. Jack glanced down. His feet were on the edge of a ridge. Below this, the earth descended into darkness. There was no way over the seemingly bottomless drop.

Suddenly, the black dog bounded forward and leapt right over the chasm, onto the lower branch of a tree, above Jack's head. The dog's weight pulled the tree branch down, until it stretched over the huge gap.
"The dog didn't seem to weigh anything on the rubble," thought Jack, "but he seems heavy now, I don't understand?"

The black dog barked. "He wants me to cross it," thought Jack. The branch didn't look very wide, but Jack took a deep breath and stepped onto it. He walked across, as slowly and carefully as he could, and every time he was about to look down, the dog barked at him. Soon, Jack was on the other side of the drop. The strange dog barked, happily.

"Thanks, you saved me," said Jack, turning to look at the dog. But the dog had gone. Jack could hear him barking in the trees up ahead, so he followed the sound.

Jack followed the barking, but could not see the dog. After a long walk, suddenly, the forest gave way to open ground. To his amazement, Jack found that he was back at his aunt and uncle's house. The dog had led him home.

Jack told Uncle Bill and Aunt Vera all about the black dog. When he had finished, they smiled and gave one another a knowing look. "We've got something to show you," they said and walked out into the garden.

Under the old willow tree, was a small headstone. "This is where Andy is buried," said Jack's uncle. "He was our dog and whenever anyone got lost in the forest, Andy always guided them back."

"That's what I was trying to tell you," said Aunt Vera, smiling. "But you always looked so bored." She pulled out a small photograph from her pocket. It was the same dog that had helped Jack in the forest.

"It was Andy that saved me," said Jack.

From that day on, Jack was never bored when he went to stay with his aunt and uncle. He would explore the forest for hours, knowing he would never get lost. Sometimes, he would see a familiar black shadow, or hear a bark from the trees. Jack always knew that Andy was somewhere out there, keeping him safe from harm.

# The Ghost Ship

Lawrence stood on the deck of the old pirate ship. It had long since left the sea and been moored in the middle of a busy theme park. His class was on a day trip and it should have been the best fun ever. The trouble was, it was turning out not to be fun at all. Ryan Twigg was trying to bully Lawrence into ringing a big bell that stood on the main deck of the great ship.

Lawrence saw the sign above the bell and it made him nervous. "Genuine bell from the real pirate ship, *The Revenge*. DO NOT RING, or you will summon the pirate ghosts," he read out loud.

"Come on, Lawrence," interrupted Ryan, "you don't want everyone to think you're a coward, do you?" There were muffled chuckles and giggles from the other children, but Lawrence didn't find it funny. What if the bell really did summon the pirate ghosts?

Suddenly, Ryan reached out and tugged at the big bell. "Run, everyone!" he cried, as he raced off, leaving Lawrence standing on the deck, holding his hands over his ears to dull the deafening sound.

The ringing stopped abruptly. Everything went quiet and a heavy silence fell. Then, Lawrence noticed that something very strange was happening.

Do Not Ring!

The deck of the ship began to shake and strange forms rose out of the wooden floor. Ragged-looking skeleton sailors appeared, wearing old-fashioned clothes. They surrounded Lawrence, their dry bones clattering as they moved.

The tallest of the pirate ghosts stepped forward. He had a skull face, rimmed with a huge, red beard. "I am Captain Redbeard of the pirate ship, *The Revenge*," he announced.

The captain swept off his wide-brimmed hat and bowed to Lawrence. "We have been cursed by a powerful sea-witch, to only be able to rise up when the ship's bell rings. We are doomed to live inside this fairground and never see the sea. That is, unless we can unlock our treasure chest." Just then, a ghostly chest rose up from the floor, locked with a gigantic padlock.

Lawrence should have been scared, but he wasn't. The sea-witch's curse seemed very unfair. "Where's the key to the lock?" he asked.
"It is out of our reach, forever," replied the captain, sadly. "It lies in the ship's hull and is guarded by a deadly, giant octopus. Only someone who does not dwell in the land of ghosts can lift the curse."

"Lawrence felt sorry for the ghost pirates. "Perhaps I could fetch the key for you?" he said.
The captain was very surprised. "You're braver than you look," he said.

Without another word, Lawrence strode over to the cabin door in the side of the ship and stepped down into the eerie gloom of the dark, wet hold below.

The rickety wooden steps were old and slimy. As he stepped down them, Lawrence saw the ghostly octopus. It had huge eyes with slit pupils and a razor-sharp beak. Its eight tentacles writhed and squirmed, dripping thick slime all over the floor. In one of its tentacles was a shiny, golden key.

Lawrence shook with fear and stepped down again, but the rotting wood gave way and he slipped. The huge, squelching body of the octopus moved closer. It's eyes grew black with anger. It raised its huge tentacles, splattering slime everywhere and tried to grab Lawrence.

Panicking and gasping for breath, Lawrence tried in vain to grab the key. He struggled, slipping on the stinking slime until the spectral octopus loomed over him, snapping its lethal beak. Lawrence thrashed and kicked with all his strength, then suddenly, he touched something hard and cold. He had managed to grab the key.

The octopus let out an unearthly scream and began to disappear. Shaking with exhaustion, Lawrence scrambled back up the steps as fast as his trembling legs could carry him.

Back on deck, Captain Redbeard unlocked the chest. Inside, piles of ghostly treasure glittered and gleamed. "We're free of the curse!" cried the captain, and all of the pirates cheered. Captain Redbeard turned to Lawrence. "You saved us all, young lad. What can we do for you before we return to the sea?"

Lawrence couldn't think of anything at first. Then he saw Ryan and his friends come on board. They had come back to see if Lawrence had got into trouble for ringing the bell. Lawrence quickly whispered something to the captain, who suddenly disappeared with his crew.

"Did you go crying to your mummy?" taunted Ryan.

Suddenly, the mist rose up from the deck. Captain Redbeard appeared, waving a huge, pirate cutlass. "Shiver me timbers!" he bellowed. "Show me the scurvy dog who does bully brave shipmate, Lawrence, and I'll run him through."

Ryan looked up in horror at the fierce pirate and his terrible sword. His lower lip quivered, as if he was about to cry, then he ran screaming from the deck, followed by his friends. Captain Redbeard chuckled, winked at Lawrence and disappeared.

After that, no one ever bullied Lawrence again and only he knew that it was all thanks to a ringing bell on a cursed ghost ship.

# Secret Spells

Rosie and Joe looked out of the window, as a strange old lady shuffled up their drive and rang the doorbell. They ran downstairs to see who it was. "Well, let me in then," they heard a shrill voice say, as their dad answered the door.

The old lady that stepped into the hallway was very thin. Her face was hard and red and she was dressed in an old, flowing dress with a red, floral design all over it. A thimble hung on a silver chain around her neck and she carried a single, saggy leather bag.

"Children, this is Aunt Elvira," said Dad, looking uncomfortable. "We haven't seen her for a very long time," he stammered, "and she has come to stay."

Aunt Elvira turned her icy gaze on Rosie and Joe. They didn't like the way she stared at them. Her eyes were cold and hard, like two green stones.

Just as Rosie and Joe had feared, having Aunt Elvira around was no fun at all. She took over Rosie's bedroom and complained about every noise the children made. They noticed, too, that their Aunt had some very strange habits.

When she thought that no one was looking, Aunt Elvira would go out into the backyard and rummage furiously among the tall flowers. She would come back in with foul-smelling weeds, as well as strange stones and sticks, which she took up to her room. It was clear to Rosie and Joe that there was something not quite right about Aunt Elvira.

One morning, Rosie and Joe were having breakfast when they looked out and saw Aunt Elvira shouting over the fence at Bill, their next-door neighbor. "Stop that dreadful whistling!" she shouted. "It's giving me a headache." "A man's allowed to whistle in his own garden," replied Bill, looking confused.

Aunt Elvira was furious. She marched back into the house and stomped up the stairs. The two children winced as she banged the bedroom door shut.

Rosie and Joe crept upstairs and Rosie looked through the keyhole of her aunt's bedroom. Inside, Aunt Elvira took the silver thimble from the chain and placed it on the floor. "Grow, thimble," she whispered, and the thimble began to swell. It pulsed and quivered and grew until it was like a small cauldron.

Aunt Elvira tossed the foul-smelling weeds into the pot and gurgled some strange words. The cauldron bubbled and spat and Aunt Elvira looked very happy indeed.

Suddenly, Bill let out a terrifying scream from the garden. Rosie and Joe raced down the stairs and out into the garden. Bill was nowhere to be seen. However, there, on the fence, was a depressed-looking toad. "That can't be Bill," said Joe, "can it?"

The toad croaked and then started whistling a sad, slow tune. "It is," said Rosie, "Aunt Elvira has turned Bill into a toad." Joe thought for a moment. "We've got to get that thimble," he said, "otherwise we'll all end up as pond life!"

That night, when everyone was asleep, Joe and Rosie crept out of bed. Trying not to think of how frightened they were, they tiptoed to Rosie's old room, where Aunt Elvira was sleeping.

They silently crept up to the door and then opened it, quietly. Aunt Elvira was lying fully clothed on the bed. She was as still as a statue and the thimble was on the silver chain round her neck.

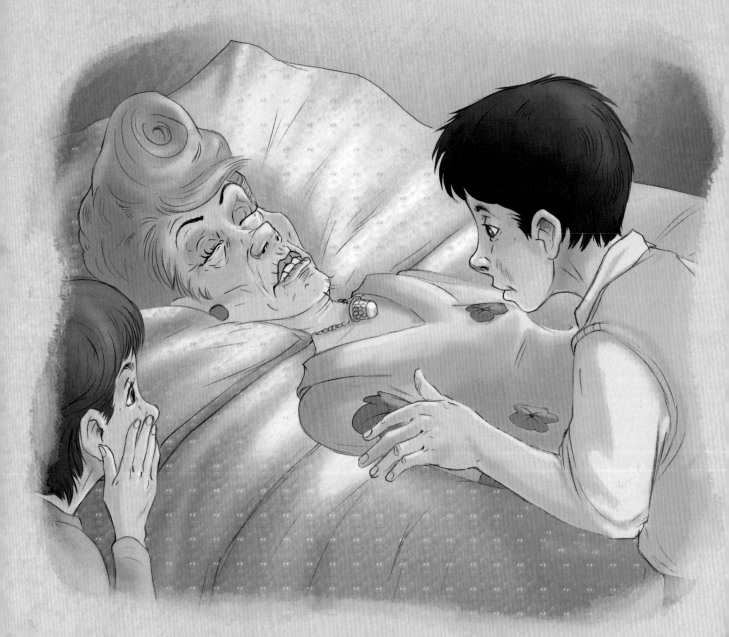

Joe reached forward to take the thimble, his hand shaking. His finger brushed against the old woman's skin and it was cold and slimy. The thimble was stuck securely to the chain and the chain had no opening on it. "It's no good," he whispered to Rosie, "I can't get it."
"You have to," insisted Rosie, "we have no choice."

Joe carefully got hold of the silver chain. He pursed his lips and closed his eyes and with one, huge yank, he pulled the chain off Aunt Elvira's neck.

The old woman shot bolt upright in bed. Her eyes glowed with rage. "THIEF!" she snarled.

"Run!" cried Joe, to Rosie. They scrambled down the stairs and fumbled with the lock on the door. Behind them, Aunt Elvira levitated down the stairs with ease.

The terrified children ran to the kitchen. In an attempt to hide the thimble, Joe threw it into the empty washing machine and closed the door. "Give me back my thimble, you brats," she screeched from the doorway.

Suddenly, Rosie had an idea. "Thimble, grow," she shouted. A strange sound came from the washing machine. The thimble was trying to grow, but there wasn't enough room. "No!" cried Aunt Elvira.

The washing machine rumbled and there was a terrible crack. The door of the machine burst open and broken bits of cauldron came flying out.

Suddenly, Aunt Elvira seemed to shrink. All the power drained out of her, until she was just a mean-looking old lady. Without another word, she ran out of the back door, wailing.

Just then, the toad hopped into the kitchen and began to grow and grow, until their neighbor, Bill, was standing there. He squinted and rubbed his eyes. "Sorry, kids," said Bill, looking confused, "I must have been sleepwalking." Rosie and Joe smiled at each other. Aunt Elvira wouldn't bother anyone ever again.

# The Lethal Laboratory

Jules and Ruby stood outside the creepy mansion, with their suitcases. They weren't too keen on the idea of spending a weekend with their eccentric, Great Uncle Bertram. However, Mum had insisted that it was about time their reclusive relative came out of his shell, so here they were.

Great Uncle Bertram appeared in the doorway with a sullen, unwelcoming grin on his face. He wore a white lab coat and had the thickest, roundest glasses they'd ever seen. His hair hung like limp noodles around his head and his tight grin made him look quite sinister.

"I suppose you had better come in," he mumbled. "I don't know why people can't just leave me alone to get on with my work."

Great Uncle Bertram continued to mutter under his breath as he showed Jules and Ruby around the dilapidated house. They had never seen anywhere so big, or so empty. Every room was bare and it was freezing cold. In the middle of the massive hall, there was a big trapdoor.

"What's down there?" asked Ruby.
"Never you mind," snapped Great Uncle Bertram, "you must never go down there, that's my laboratory. Now off to bed with you, I have work to do."

That night, after a supper of stale bread and cold baked beans, Rosie and Joe went to bed. Huge moths flapped in the moonlight and spiders scuttled up the walls. Downstairs, strange groans came from Uncle Bertram's laboratory.

The next morning, Jules and Ruby asked Great Uncle Bertram about the strange noises in the night. Their uncle turned purple with rage. "Don't ask me questions and keep your noses out of my laboratory," he warned.

"Something is under that trapdoor in the hall," said Ruby when their great uncle went down into his laboratory, "and whatever it is, it wants to get out. I think we should go down there tonight and find out what's going on."

That night, when they were sure Great Uncle Bertram was asleep, Jules and Ruby crept downstairs and through the trapdoor. Bottles of dangerous-looking chemicals bubbled and smoked on a large table. A huge electricity generator sparked and fizzed in one corner.

In the centre of the room, a motionless creature was chained to a large slab. It looked a bit like an ape and a bit like a man, but with large, furred ears like a wolf and big, pointed horns like a stag. "I think it's dead," said Jules. He poked the creature and the monster sat up, suddenly, with a deep grunt.

Jules and Ruby screamed as the monster twisted and struggled. It groaned and yanked at the chains until, finally, they snapped.

The creature jumped off the slab and came towards Jules and Ruby, who cowered in a corner. The grunting noises got louder. Suddenly, Jules realized that the monster wasn't trying to harm them, it was trying to say something to them. Its cries sounded almost like speech.

"Help me," said the beast, in a strange, gurgling voice. It held out its hands. "I was captured in the forest. Please set me free."

Ruby and Jules looked at each other. The poor creature looked so sad. Ruby put her hand out and the creature took it in its huge paw.

Cautiously, the children crept up the steps and opened the trapdoor. It made a horrible creak that seemed to echo around the house.

Ruby tried to open the locked front door. The creature raised its huge paws to smash it, but Ruby stopped him. "Sssh, you'll wake Great Uncle Bertram," she hissed.

Meanwhile, Jules went to check that Great Uncle Bertram was still asleep. He opened his bedroom door to see moonlight shining on an empty bed. Jules quickly rushed back down the stairs. "We have to get back to the lab, quickly," he gasped.

Ruby and the creature hurried through the trapdoor, but as they reached the laboratory, a steel cage fell down around them, with a gigantic crash. "So, you have found my creature," said Great Uncle Bertram with a malicious laugh. "Do not try to escape, the bars of the cage are electrified."

Great Uncle Bertram explained how he had captured the beast in the woods. "I knew its discovery would make me the most famous scientist in the world," he said with a sly, greedy smile.

Ruby could see that Jules was creeping slowly down the stairs behind Great Uncle Bertram. Suddenly, Jules leaped forward and gave his uncle such a shove, he fell against the electrified bars of the cage. The uncle's hair stood on end and his eyes bulged in the most peculiar way.

Jules rushed over and pulled the lever so that the bars of the cage lifted. Ruby and the creature stumbled out and followed Jules back up the steps and into the hallway.

Once in the hall, the beast ran to the door and with one mighty blow, he smashed it down and fled into the woods. "Thank you, friends," he cried as he disappeared into the dark forest. Ruby and Jules turned to see two bright car headlights coming up the drive towards them.

"It's Mum and Dad!" cried Ruby, rushing into the arms of her father. "We just thought we would come and see how you are doing," said Mum. "Great Uncle Bertram can be a bit unpredictable, sometimes."

Ruby and Jules looked at each other. Then they looked at the scowling figure of Great Uncle Bertram, who had recovered and staggered outside. "Yes, we know," they said.

Mum shook her head. "Poor Uncle," she sighed. "He really does have such terrible hair. I think we'd better leave him alone with his experiments."

"What a good idea," said Ruby and Jules, as they waved goodbye to Great Uncle Bertram and the lethal laboratory, forever.